There's a Pig up my Nose!

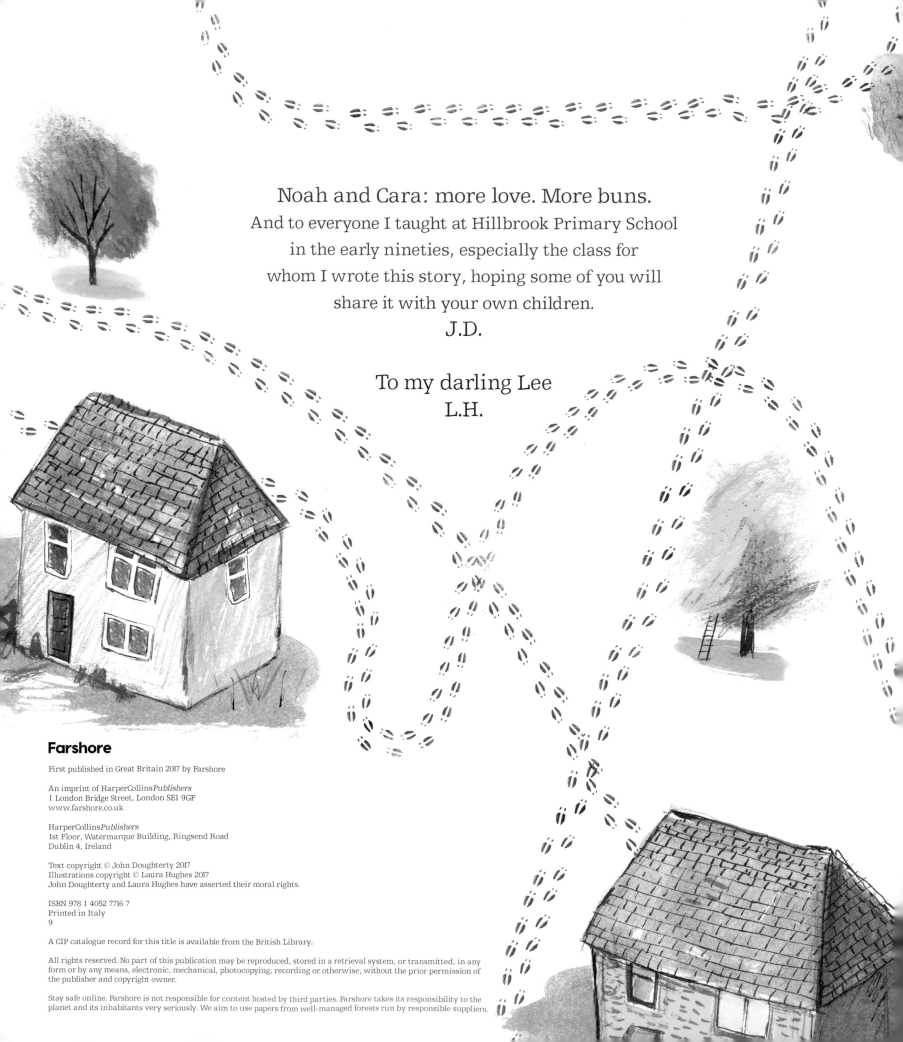

Noah and Cara: more love. More buns.
And to everyone I taught at Hillbrook Primary School
in the early nineties, especially the class for
whom I wrote this story, hoping some of you will
share it with your own children.
J.D.

To my darling Lee
L.H.

Farshore

First published in Great Britain 2017 by Farshore

An imprint of HarperCollins*Publishers*
1 London Bridge Street, London SE1 9GF
www.farshore.co.uk

HarperCollins*Publishers*
1st Floor, Watermarque Building, Ringsend Road
Dublin 4, Ireland

Text copyright © John Doughterty 2017
Illustrations copyright © Laura Hughes 2017
John Doughterty and Laura Hughes have asserted their moral rights.

ISBN 978 1 4052 7716 7
Printed in Italy
9

A CIP catalogue record for this title is available from the British Library.

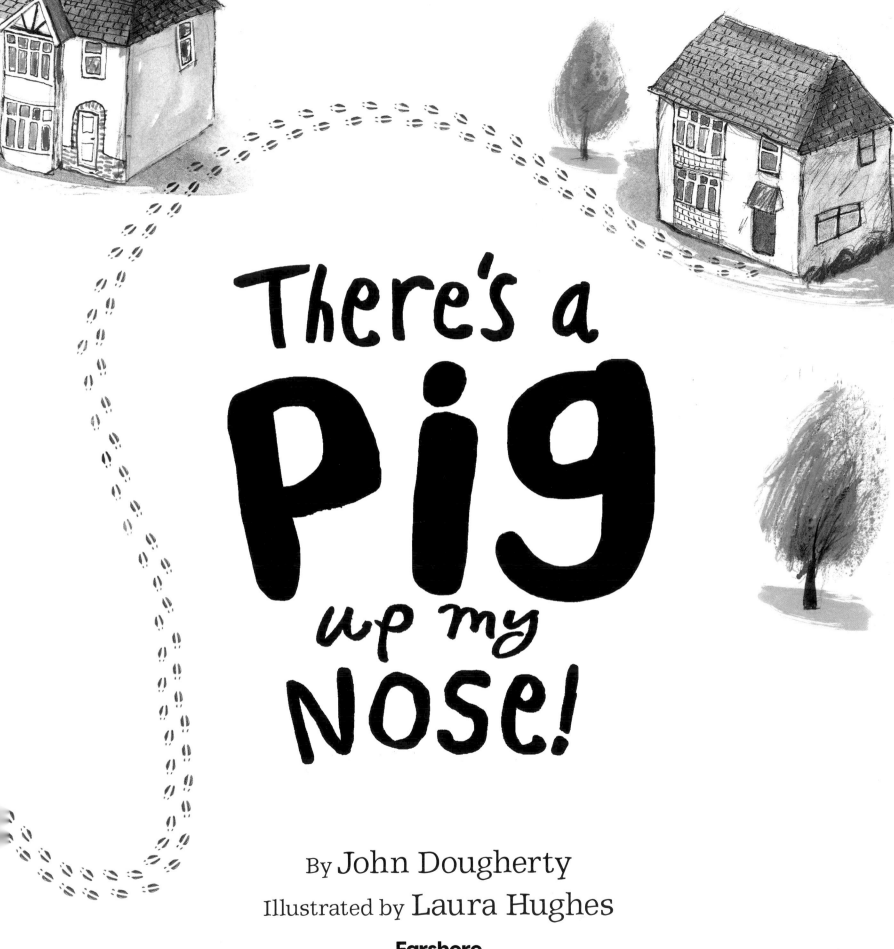

There's a Pig up my Nose!

By John Dougherty

Illustrated by Laura Hughes

Farshore

One night, when Natalie was
fast asleep, a pig trotted into the house,

up the stairs,

into Natalie's bedroom . . .

. . . and up her nose.

Next morning, Natalie bounced out of bed
and trotted down to breakfast.

"Morning, Squidge," said her dad.
"Did you sleep well?"

"Yes, thanks,"
said Natalie.

"OINK!" went Natalie's nose.

"Oh my goodness!" said Natalie's mum. "She's got some strange disease. We need to take her to the doctor!"

The doctor tapped
Natalie's knee,

looked at her tongue,

took her temperature,

listened to her chest . . .

. . . and popped a camera up her nose.

"There's the problem," he said. "She's not ill.
She's just got **a pig up her nose.**"

That morning was not
a very good one for
Mrs Daffodil's class.

The children tried their best to be quiet, but every time they settled down to work, Natalie's nose would go

OINK!

and disturb them.

It went at playtime and spoiled the game of hide-and-seek.

It went

during the story and spoiled the exciting bit.

After lunch, Mrs Daffodil said, "This afternoon we're not going to do games after all."

"Oh-wuh!"

went all the children.

"Instead," Mrs Daffodil went on, "I want you to invent a way of getting a pig out of Natalie's nose."

"Hooray!" went all the children.

OINK!

went Natalie's nose.

The children all worked very hard.

Sophie and Krystina wanted to push a big hooked stick up Natalie's nose and pull the pig out.

Natalie didn't like that idea.

Sean, Alex and Daniel wanted to stick a vacuum cleaner up Natalie's nose and suck the pig out.

Natalie didn't like that idea either.

Kylie and Kim thought the pig might come out if they held Natalie upside-down and hit her on the head with a large inflatable rhinoceros.

Natalie **definitely** didn't like that idea.

Then Mark and Joseph explained their idea.
It was **much** better.

They got a big pepper pot from the
dinner ladies and shook it all
over Natalie's nose.

Aa ...

aaa...

aaaaaa...

Next morning, Natalie bounced
out of bed and ambled
down to breakfast.

"Morning, Squidge!" said her dad.
"I hope there isn't a pig up your nose today!"

"No," replied Natalie. "There isn't
a pig up my nose."